3 1833 02445 4688

P9-EEN-141

JE
KING, CHRISTOPHER, 1945-
THE VEGETABLES GO TO BED

**DO NOT REMOVE
CARDS FROM POCKET**

5/94

**ALLEN COUNTY PUBLIC LIBRARY
FORT WAYNE, INDIANA 46802**

You may return this book to any agency, branch,

or bookmobile of the Allen County Public Library.

DEMCO

THE VEGETABLES GO TO BED

BY **Christopher King**

ILLUSTRATED BY **Mary GrandPré**

CROWN PUBLISHERS, INC. ◆ New York

Text copyright © 1994 by Christopher L. King
Illustrations copyright © 1994 by Mary GrandPré

All rights reserved. No part of this book may be
reproduced or transmitted in any form or by any
means, electronic or mechanical, including
photocopying, recording, or by any information
storage and retrieval system, without permission
in writing from the publisher.

Published by Crown Publishers, Inc.,
a Random House company, 201 East 50th Street,
New York, New York 10022

CROWN is a trademark of Crown Publishers, Inc.
Manufactured in Singapore

Library of Congress Cataloging-in-Publication Data
King, Christopher, 1945 -
The vegetables go to bed / by Christopher L. King ;
illustrated by Mary GrandPré.
Summary: The tomatoes, carrots, spinach plants,
and other vegetables in the garden prepare to go
to bed, each in its own fashion.
[1. Bedtime—Fiction. 2. Vegetables—Fiction. 3.
Stories in rhyme.] I. Grandpre, Mary, ill. II. Title.
PZ8.3K568Ve 1994
[E]—dc20   92-27650

ISBN 0-517-59125-1 (trade)
     0-517-59126-X (lib. bdg.)

10 9 8 7 6 5 4 3 2 1   First Edition

For Chitra,
my favorite gardening partner.
                         C. K.

To Mom and Dad
and the Hawka-bird and
Chincha-bug.
                    M. G.

Allen County Public Library
900 Webster Street
PO Box 2270
Fort Wayne, IN 46801-2270

Shhh! The vegetables are going to bed.

Every pea and carrot,

Every head of lettuce,

Cabbage, bean, and brussels sprout

Will be tucked in

Before the stars come out.

Plump tomatoes wash their ruddy cheeks with dew,

And so should you.

Cornstalks in the evening rain have bathed their tender ears.

Corncobs snuggle up in corn silk

Till the sun appears.

But lettuces are restless and won't say the day is done,

Until the summer wind has come

And gently kissed each one.

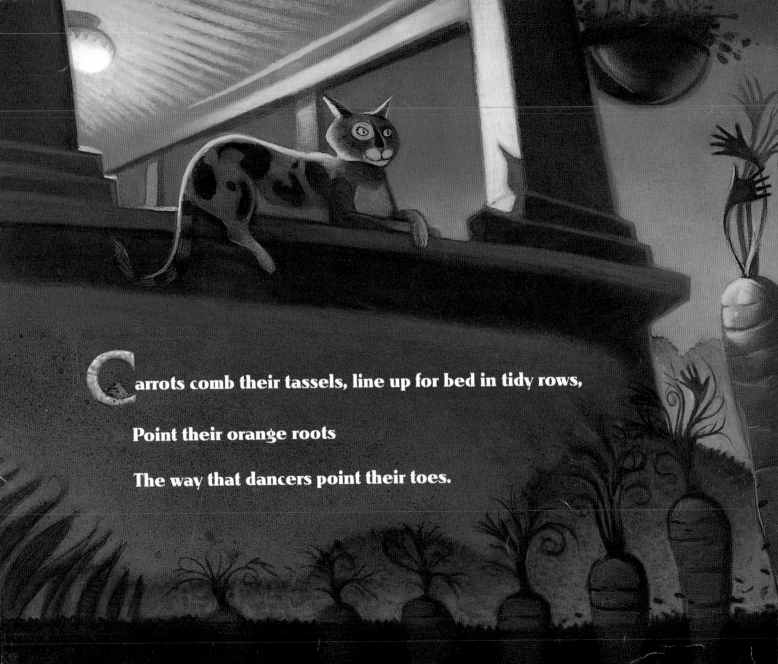

Carrots comb their tassels, line up for bed in tidy rows,

Point their orange roots

The way that dancers point their toes.

The onions have been crying:

"We don't want to go to sleep!"

But they're nice and cozy now

And much too tired to weep.

One by one, potatoes close their eyes,

Listening to the sound of bells,

The peppers' lullabies.

Sleepy spinach plants give one last wave with leafy hands,

Before they drift away

To dreams of wild green wonderlands.

All around the garden, the marigolds stand guard.

No hungry bug or beetle

Dares steal into their yard.

Outside your window,

The sun turns off the light.

Good night, you vegetables.

Good night! Good night!

Robin walks the rows to make sure everyone's in bed,

Pulls a worm up in his bill,

Cocks his head,

Now all is still.

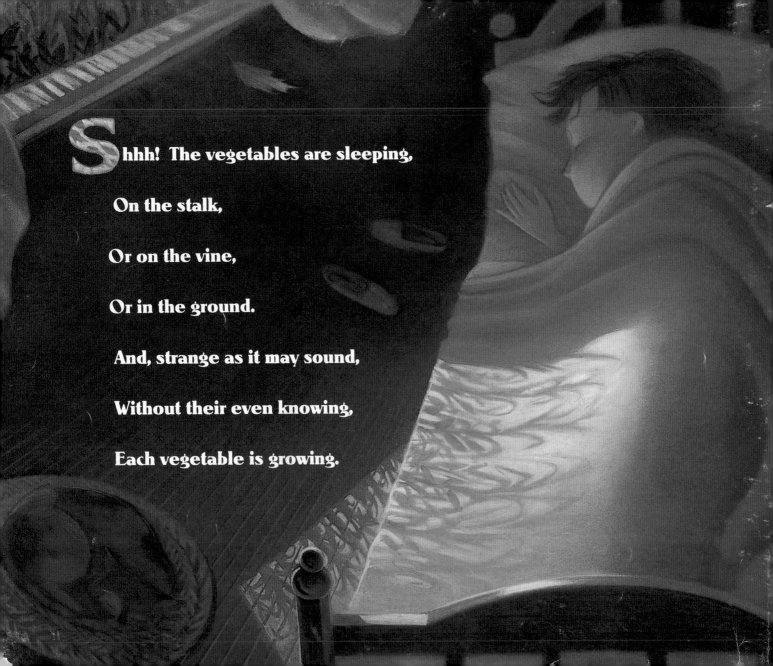

Shhh! The vegetables are sleeping,

On the stalk,

Or on the vine,

Or in the ground.

And, strange as it may sound,

Without their even knowing,

Each vegetable is growing.